Orange You Glad It's Halloween, Amber Brown?

PAULA DANZIGER

Illustrated by Tony Ross

G. P. Putnam's Sons · New York

Look for all of the A **is for Amber** *titles*

It's Justin Time, Amber Brown

What a Trip, Amber Brown

It's a Fair Day, Amber Brown

Get Ready for Second Grade, Amber Brown

Second Grade Rules, Amber Brown

Orange You Glad It's Halloween, Amber Brown?

G. P. PUTNAM'S SONS
A division of Penguin Young Readers Group. Published by The Penguin Group.

PENGUIN GROUP (USA) INC., 375 Hudson Street, New York, NY 10014, U.S.A. PENGUIN GROUP (CANADA), 10 Alcorn Avenue, Toronto, Ontario, Canada M4V 3B2 (a division of Pearson Penguin Canada Inc.) PENGUIN BOOKS LTD, 80 Strand, London WC2R 0RL, England. PENGUIN IRELAND, 25 St. Stephen's Green, Dublin 2, Ireland (a division of Penguin Books Ltd.) PENGUIN BOOKS INDIA PVT LTD, 11 Community Centre, Panchsheel Park, New Delhi - 110 017, India. PENGUIN GROUP (NZ), Cnr Airborne and Rosedale Roads, Albany, Auckland, New Zealand (a division of Pearson New Zealand Ltd). PENGUIN BOOKS (SOUTH AFRICA) (PTY) LTD, 24 Sturdee Avenue, Rosebank, Johannesburg 2196, South Africa. PENGUIN BOOKS LTD, Registered Offices: 80 Strand, London WC2R 0RL, England.

Designed by Gunta Alexander. Text set in Calisto.

Library of Congress Cataloging-in-Publication Data

Danziger, Paula, 1944– Orange you glad it's Halloween, Amber Brown? / Paula Danziger ; illustrated by Tony Ross. p. cm. — (A is for Amber) Summary: Amber Brown and her classmates celebrate Halloween, while Amber wonders if her parents' arguing will ruin the holiday for her. [1. Halloween—Fiction. 2. Schools—Fiction. 3. Fighting (Psychology) Fiction.] I. Title: Orange you glad it is Halloween, Amber Brown?. II. Ross, Tony, ill. III. Title. PZ7.D2394Or 2005 [Fic]—dc22 2003026637 ISBN 0-399-23471-3   10 9 8 7 6 5 4 3   First Impression

To Susan Kochan —P. D.

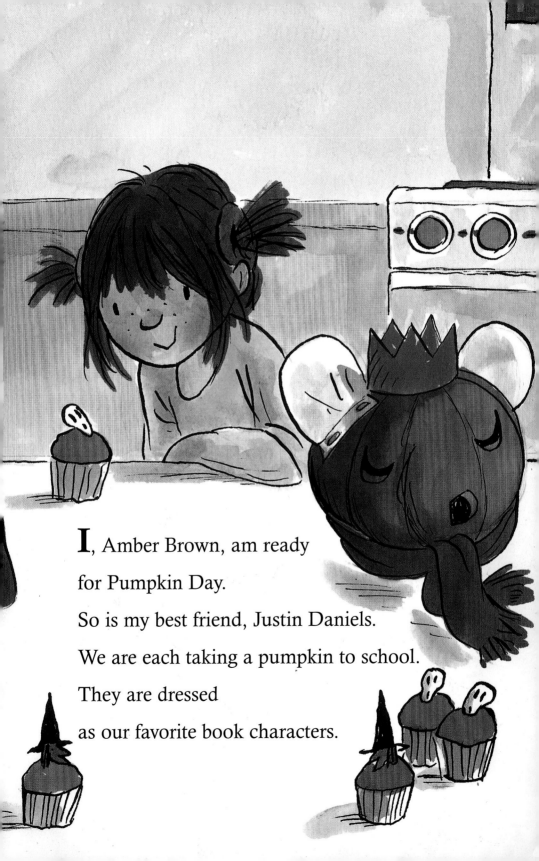

I, Amber Brown, am ready
for Pumpkin Day.
So is my best friend, Justin Daniels.
We are each taking a pumpkin to school.
They are dressed
as our favorite book characters.

My parents are in the living room,

having a talk.

Something tells me it is not a happy talk.

They have not been getting along lately.

I hope that they make up before tonight.

I, Amber Brown, will be wearing

the best costume ever.

It will be a sad Halloween

if my parents are not getting along.

Justin takes his pumpkin out of the bag.

He lifts it up over his head.

The pumpkin has underpants tacked to it.

"Captain Underpants to the rescue!"

he shouts.

The underpants cover part of Justin's face.

There is pumpkin juice on them.

"Are we going soon?" Justin makes a face.

I sigh. "I hope so."

I want to cry.

Justin puts his pumpkin in front of his face.

"Knock, knock."

"Who's there?" I ask.

"Banana."

"Banana who?" I ask.

Justin says "Banana" again.

"Banana who?" I ask again.

That happens three more times.

I, Amber Brown, am getting tired

of bananas.

Finally Justin yells, "KNOCK, KNOCK!"

I glare. "Who is there. You better tell me."

Justin screams, "ORANGE."

"ORANGE WHO?" I yell back.

"Orange you glad it's Halloween,

Amber Brown?"

I giggle and nod.

I will be very glad that it's Halloween

if my parents don't ruin it.

That would be a bad trick,

not a good treat.

My dad rushes into the room.

"Hurry up, kids . . . or you're going to be late."

That's not our fault, I think.

My mom comes into the kitchen.

She smiles at Justin and me.

I can't tell if everything is okay or not.

I wish I knew.

She kisses me good-bye.

Justin asks her to kiss

Captain Underpants good-bye.

She does.

Then she kisses Justin.

She doesn't kiss my dad.

Dad picks up the cupcakes

that Mom and I baked last night.

Justin, Dad and I go out to the car.

Justin and Captain Underpants and I

sit in the backseat.

My pumpkin, Lily, her purple plastic purse,

and the cupcakes sit in the front with Dad.

"Amber," Justin asks,

"what are you going to be for Halloween?"

"It's a surprise," I say.

"I'm not telling anyone,

not even you."

Justin sticks his tongue out at me.

"Well . . . I'm not going to tell you mine either,"

he says. "You are probably going

as a giant booger."

I giggle. But I don't tell him.

We get to the school and rush inside.

A pumpkin-head is standing by the counter.

It is wearing a sign.

It's Mr. Robinson, our principal.

He signs our late passes.

We hurry to class.

Ms. Light is already teaching.

Justin and I sit down at our desks.
Dad puts the cupcakes
on the work table and leaves.

16

Ms. Light passes out papers.

I look at mine.

Five pumpkins are drawn on the page.

We have to add eyes, noses,

mouths and teeth on each pumpkin.

We also have to add one more thing.

I give my pumpkins twenty freckles each.

Then Ms. Light asks,

"How many noses are there all together?

How many eyes? How many mouths,

teeth and other items?"

She can't fool me.

This is supposed to be fun,

but it's really math.

I look over at Justin.

He's already finished.

I look at his paper.

He has given his pumpkins pimples.

I wonder what it would look like

if a pumpkin had its pimple squeezed.

I try counting everything again.

Hannah Burton is sitting across from me.

She whispers,

"1, 2, 11, 15, 7, 62 and 3," over and over,

just to mix me up.

Hannah Burton is a pumpkin pimple.

Ms. Light comes over.

She looks at my paper.

She knows I am having trouble.

She shows me how to add it up.

I put my head down on the desk.

She rumples my hair and says,

"Don't worry. You'll be able to do this.

After all, you are one of my BRIGHT LIGHTS."

Next, each of us stands up
and tells about our pumpkin
and the book it comes from.

22

At lunch, Justin tries to make me tell
what costume I will wear tonight.
I, Amber Brown, will NOT tell him.

After lunch, Ms. Light reads us
Space Case by Edward and James Marshall.
Everyone laughs. It's really funny.
A real alien from outer space
goes trick-or-treating.

I think about tonight.

What if my parents are in a bad mood?

What if they don't do the things

we always do on Halloween?

All of a sudden, I feel sad.

What if my parents get a divorce?

Then Ms. Light says,

"Time for pumpkin jokes."

Hannah raises her hand quickly.

Ms. Light calls on her.

"How can you fix a broken pumpkin?"

Hannah asks. Then she says,

"With a pumpkin patch."

I, Amber Brown, raise my hand

even higher than Hannah raised hers.

"What's black and white and orange
and waddles?" I ask.

Nobody can guess.

"A penguin with a pumpkin!" I giggle.

Justin jumps up and down.

"Why did the pumpkin cross the road?"

Before anyone can even answer, he yells,

"Because the chicken took the day off

to trick-or-treat!!!"

Everyone tells a joke.

Then it's Pumpkin Party time
with pumpkin soup, cupcakes,
cookies, bread and pies.

School ends. We line up to leave.

Ms. Light hands each of us

a little bag of candy pumpkins and candy corn.

Justin offers me pieces of candy

if I tell him what my costume is.

I won't tell him.

Justin's mom picks us up.

We get into the backseat

with his little brother, Danny.

I think that Danny is going to be

a dirty diaper for Halloween . . .

either that or he needs a change.

Justin and I sing pumpkin songs
all the way home.

When we get to the Daniels' house,

Justin and I use our candy corn as fangs.

We pretend to be werewolves

to scare Danny.

Danny grabs one of the candy corns
out of Justin's mouth and eats it.
I bet that there is Justin slobber
on the corn!

The doorbell rings.

It's my mom.

We walk home.

There's a package on our front porch steps.

I run up and take a look at it.

We've been "ghosted"!

There's a plastic pumpkin filled with candy.

There's a piece of paper on the present.

A ghost is drawn on the page.

There's a note on the ghost:

Your house has been visited by

the friendly Halloween ghost.

Put this picture of the ghost in your window and

then secretly deliver treats and a copy of

this note to two houses in your neighborhood.

You must do this without being seen!!!

Choose houses that do not have

ghosts in their windows!

And then you can enjoy

your treats.

Happy Halloween!

I, Amber Brown, love ghosting.

Mom and I get two treat bags ready.

She and I sneak up to the Daniels' house.

We put the package on their steps.

We ring the doorbell and run away.

Then we sneak over to Kelsea Allin's house.

Kelsea is a really nice seventh-grader.

Sometimes she lets me walk her dog.

We leave the second treat there

and rush back to our house.

We fill a large bowl with regular-size candy.

I'm glad that Mom didn't buy

"Fun Size" candy.

What is fun about a little piece of candy?

Big bars are best.

Mrs. Swallow, on the next block,

gives out raisins and toothbrushes.

No one goes to her house anymore.

Dad comes home.

He is wearing light-up pumpkin boppers
on his head.

He is also carrying flowers for Mom.

"I'm sorry," Dad says.

Mom sighs, looks at me,

and then smiles at Dad.

They hug.

I, Amber Brown, am so happy.

We sit down for an early dinner.

Macaroni and cheese, carrots,

orange juice and an orange cupcake.

Orange I glad it's Halloween dinner!

I eat quickly.

I want to hurry up

and get dressed in my new costume.

But dinner is taking a long time

because the doorbell rings a lot.

Each time we all get up

to look at the costumes

and to give out treats.

Chuckie Richetti is dressed as a baseball card.

That is my second-favorite costume.

My first favorite will be my costume,

once I put it on.

My parents are smiling a lot.

They are smiling at the trick-or-treaters,

at me, at each other.

I am very happy.

I am very ready to get dressed

for Halloween.

Finally, dinner is finished.

Justin and his dad arrive.

Justin is dressed as a chicken.

He is wearing a big sign.

Why did the chicken cross the street ???
To get his Yummy Halloween treat! !! !! !! !! !! !! !! !!

I get it.

Justin is A CHICKEN JOKE!

I rush upstairs.

Mom helps me put on my costume.

She made it for me.

I go downstairs again and yell,

"SURPRISE!!!"

I, Amber Brown, am

"Eye, Amber Brown."

This is going to be

the most wonderful Halloween ever.